ON LINE

THE LITTLEST DUCKLING

By Gail Herman   Illustrated by Ann Schweninger

VIKING

VIKING
Published by the Penguin Group
Penguin Books USA Inc., 375 Hudson Street, New York, New York 10014, U.S.A.
Penguin Books Ltd, 27 Wrights Lane, London W8 5TZ, England
Penguin Books Australia Ltd, Ringwood, Victoria, Australia
Penguin Books Canada Ltd, 10 Alcorn Avenue, Toronto, Ontario, Canada M4V 3B2
Penguin Books (N.Z.) Ltd, 182–190 Wairau Road, Auckland 10, New Zealand

Penguin Books Ltd, Registered Offices: Harmondsworth, Middlesex, England

First published in 1996 by Viking, a division of Penguin Books USA Inc.

1 3 5 7 9 10 8 6 4 2

Text copyright © Gail Herman, 1996
Illustrations copyright © Ann Schweninger, 1996
All rights reserved

ISBN 0-670-85113-2

Manufactured in China
Set in Stone Sans

For my mother, with love
— G.H.

For Tracy
— A.S.

In a very small clearing, in a very small wood, by a very small pond, a mama duck stretched her wings and looked up at the sky.

"What a beautiful sunny morning," she said to her ducklings. "What should we do today?"

"Let's look for bread crumbs," said the first little duckling.

"Let's gather grass for the nest," said the second little duckling.

"Let's play in the meadow," said the third little duckling.

But the littlest duckling of all was still fast asleep,
tucked under a cozy blanket of leaves.

"Wake up, my little duckling," the mama duck said gently. "What would you like to do on this beautiful summer day?"

"Swim in the pond?" asked the littlest duckling.

"Yes!" said the first little duckling, the second little duckling, and the third little duckling, too. "Let's swim in the pond!"

So one, two, three little ducklings lined up behind their mama. Waddle, waddle. Quack, quack. Off they went, one, two, three little ducklings and the littlest one all the way at the end.

Waddle, waddle. Quack, quack.

"Are all my little ducklings here?" asked the mama duck.

"I'm here," said the first little duckling.

"I'm here," said the second little duckling.

"I'm here," said the third little duckling.

And the last little duckling called out, "I'm here, too."

One, two, three little ducklings and the littlest one, too, followed their mama over twisty old tree roots . . .

through tall green grass . . .

and through wildflowers bending in the breeze.

They followed their mama until they came to a beach made of nice soft sand, right at the edge of a cool, green pond.

Waddle, waddle. Quack, quack.

They went—splash!—into the pond.

All day long, the ducklings paddled around and around.

The first little duckling chased the waves.

The second little duckling dove down, down, down into the cool water. Then he swam up, up, up to the top.

The third little duckling played hide-and-seek in and out of the lily pads.

And the last little duckling? He floated lazily about the pond, gazing up at the clouds.

Finally it was time to go back to the nest.

"Come, my little ducklings," called their mama from the shore.

"I'm coming," said the first little duckling.

"I'm coming," said the second little duckling.

"I'm coming," said the third little duckling.

And the last little duckling said, "I'm coming, too."

But instead, that last little duckling swam around the pond once more, gazing up at the clouds.

The littlest duckling looked toward shore.

Waddle, waddle. Quack, quack.
The last little duckling followed behind . . .

across the beach made of nice soft sand . . .

through wildflowers bending in the breeze . . .

and through tall green grass. . . .

And over twisty old tree roots . . .

"Are all my little ducklings here?" asked the mama duck.

"I'm here," said the first little duckling.
"I'm here," said the second little duckling.
"I'm here," said the third little duckling.
And the last little duckling said, "I'm here, too!"

One, two, three little ducklings—and the last little duckling too—all snuggled deep into their nest. And in the very small clearing, in the very small wood, by the very small pond, the mama duck said, "Good night."